The Conflict Resolution Library™

Dealing with Rules at Home

• Elizabeth Vogel •

The Rosen Publishing Group's
PowerKids Press™
New York

Published in 2000 by The Rosen Publishing Group, Inc.
29 East 21st Street, New York, NY 10010

Photo Illustrations by Shalhevet Moshe

First Edition

Layout and design: Erin McKenna

Vogel, Elizabeth.
    Dealing with rules at home / by Elizabeth Vogel.
            p.   cm. — (The conflict resolution library)
    Includes index.
    ISBN 0-8239-5411-0 (lib. bdg.)
    1. Parent and child—United States—Juvenile literature. 2. Discipline of children—United States—Juvenile literature. I. Title. II. Series.
    HQ755.85.V64 1999
    306.874'3—dc21   98-50349
                                                                    CIP
                                                                    AC

Manufactured in the United States of America

Contents

What Are Rules?

There are rules at home, rules at school, and rules to follow in the games and sports that you play. Rules let you know what you can and cannot do. The first place you learn about rules is in your home. Different families sometimes have different rules, but all families have them. Some rules might be harder to follow than others. Maybe you do not like all the rules in your house. This can be **frustrating**. However, rules are important and are there to help you.

◀ *This girl helps her mom with the dishes after dinner. This is one of the household rules.*

Who Makes Rules?

Parents, grandparents, or other **trusted** adults probably make the rules in your family. This is because they have had many years of **experience**. Adults make rules so that you can learn what to do in certain situations. Rules about table manners at home teach you how to act when you go to a friend's house for lunch. Adults also make rules to keep you safe. A rule that says you cannot go swimming when no adults are around is a good example. This rule could stop you from getting into an accident.

Learning table manners is a common rule in many households. ▶

Common Household Rules

Some rules are common in many households. Rules about cleaning your room and putting away your toys probably sound familiar to you. These rules keep your home neat. If you own a cat, there might be rules about cleaning the litter box. Bedtime rules are common, too. Going to bed at the same time each night helps you wake up feeling good. Another rule that is important is to know your phone number and home address by memory. Knowing your phone number and address can be very helpful in an **emergency**.

◀ *This girl's family has a rule about making the beds each morning. Maybe your family does, too.*

Leo and Syd

Syd wanted to go skateboarding with his friends after school. Syd's brother Leo wanted to join them, but he knew he shouldn't. Leo and Syd were supposed to go right home after school. "Let's go!" shouted Syd, but Leo did not want to break the rule. When Leo arrived home, his grandparents were there for a visit with the boys. They were upset that Syd had not come home with Leo. Syd got in trouble when he finally did get home. He learned that there was a good reason for this rule about coming home after school.

Leo did not let his brother talk him into breaking a rule. Leo went home right after school. ▶

When You Don't Like Rules

Do you feel frustrated with the rules in your home? Maybe you think some of the rules are unfair. Some rules can be changed or improved. Talk to your parents. Suggest a way to change the rule you don't like to something that might work better. Your parents may be willing to change the rule for a short time to see how it works. Sometimes, though, there is a good reason why the rules have to stay the way they are. Having a discussion is one way to learn more about the rules in your home.

◀ *If you are unhappy about a rule, it's a good idea to talk about it with your parents.*

Roberto and Grandpa

Roberto just moved in with his grandparents. Their rules are different from his parents' rules. Every time Grandpa asks him to take the garbage out, Roberto gets upset. He tells Grandpa how he feels. Grandpa explains that since they live in the city, they have to be careful that bugs don't find their garbage. Grandpa decides that they can **compromise**. If Roberto takes the garbage out in the morning, Grandpa will take it out at night. Roberto is glad he told Grandpa his feelings about this rule.

Roberto talked to Grandpa about the garbage rule, and they came up with a good plan. ▶

When You Break Rules

What happens when you break a rule? Usually, there is a **consequence**. A consequence is something that happens because of what you did. If you don't follow the rules, one consequence might be that your parents will be upset with you. You might lose a **privilege**. Maybe you won't be allowed to have ice cream because you didn't clean up your toys. Maybe you won't get to go to your best friend's party because you didn't rake the leaves. Losing a privilege often helps people remember to follow the rules.

◄ *This boy broke a rule in his house and has to accept the consequence. He is not allowed to have dessert.*

Angela's Bedtime

Angela was supposed to go to bed at eight o'clock, but instead she stayed awake, reading. The next morning she was tired when she went to her soccer game. Angela played **goalie**. At first her team was winning by one point. Then Angela let two goals go by her. Her team lost. Angela knew she had not played well because she had been so sleepy. She learned the consequences of not following the rules. That night, Angela was ready for bed at exactly eight o'clock. She wanted to be well rested for the next day's game.

If Angela hadn't broken her bedtime rule, she might have played better during her soccer game. ▶

Why People Break Rules

There are many reasons people might break rules. Sometimes people break rules because they want more attention. Other times someone breaks a rule as a shortcut when he is in a hurry to do something. Maybe you want to break a rule because your friends or your brother and sister dare you to do it. You might want to impress them or show them that you're cool by breaking the rule. Instead, tell them no. You can choose to follow the rules.

◀ *Even if someone tries to get you to break the rules, it is up to you to follow the rules.*

Following Rules

Sometimes you might feel that rules are not fun. Rules can be hard to follow, but they can also teach you how to behave with other people. If everyone learned how to follow the rules, then people could get along better. Kids and adults have rules they need to learn. When you know the rules, you know what people expect from you. Rules help you know what to expect from your family, too. You know when it's time to take your dog for a walk or empty the trash cans. Having rules at home helps to make every day a good day!

Glossary

compromise (KOM-pruh-myz) When people work out an argument by each giving in a little.

consequence (KON-suh-kwens) Something that happens because of something you did.

emergency (ih-MUR-jin-see) An event that happens with little or no warning, where help is needed very fast.

experience (ik-SPIR-ee-ents) Knowledge or skill gained by doing or seeing things.

frustrating (FRUS-tray-ting) When not being able to change a situation makes you feel angry or sad.

goalie (GO-lee) The person on a soccer team who stands in the goal and blocks the ball to keep the other team from scoring.

privilege (PRIHV-lij) A special right or favor.

trusted (TRUS-tid) When someone or something can be depended on.

Index